USBORNE CASTLE TALES

THE TOURNAMENT

Heather Amery
Illustrated by Stephen Cartwright

Language consultant: Betty Root
Series editor: Jenny Tyler

There is a little yellow duck to find on every page.

This is Grey Stone Castle.

This is King Leo and Queen Rose. They have two children called Prince Max and Princess Alice.

Today everyone is busy.

"What's happening?" says Max. "I'm having a grand tournament tomorrow," says the King.

"What's a tournament?" asks Alice.

"Knights on horses fight each other," says the King. "It will happen down there on the field."

"I'm going on my pony."

"I'm going to play at being a knight," says
Max. He runs to the stables. Alice follows him.

"Can I come?" asks Alice.

"No," says Max. "Only boys can be knights."
He gets on his pony and rides away.

Alice runs to Max's bedroom.

She puts on Max's old clothes and a cap over
her hair. "Now I look like a boy," she says.

Alice goes to the stables.

She gets on a pony and rides down to the field. Max is pretending to be a knight.

"Come and play," says a boy.

"You can play at being a knight. You must have a helmet, a shield and a wooden lance."

"What's your name?"

"Um, it's Alex," Alice tells the boy. She puts on the helmet. "Here's your shield," says the boy.

"Come on, come and fight."

A big boy shouts at Alice. Alice rides up to
the rails and holds up her lance and shield.

"I'll knock you off."

The big boy shouts. He rides at Alice. He tries to hit her with his lance. But he misses her.

Alice swings her lance.

She hits the big boy when he rides past.
He falls off his pony. "I've won!" shouts Alice.

"It's my turn."

"Come and fight me," shouts Max. But Alice's pony stumbles and Alice falls off.

The King and Queen come and look.

"Is that boy hurt?" asks the Queen. She takes off Alice's helmet. "Oh, it's Alice!" she says.

The King picks up Alice.

"You're a very naughty girl," says the Queen.
"You're a brave little knight," says the King.